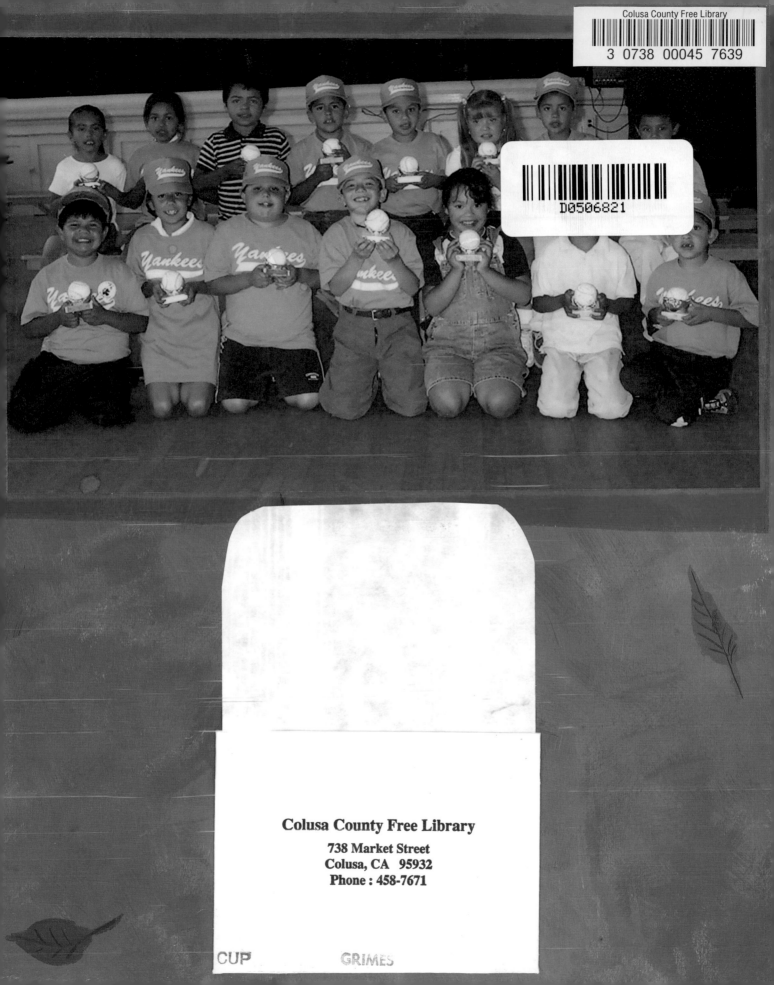

For Jess, John and Ollie
~ C.L.

For Glen P.
~ T.W.

First published in the United States 1997 by
Little Tiger Press,
12221 West Feerick Street, Wauwatosa, WI 53222
Originally published in Great Britain 1997 by
Magi Publications, London
Text © 1997 Christine Leeson
Illustrations © 1997 Tim Warnes
All rights reserved.
Library of Congress Cataloging-in-Publication Data
Leeson, Christine, 1965-
Davy's scary journey / by Christine Leeson;
illustrated by Tim Warnes.
p.   cm.
Summary : Davy the duckling ventures on a scary
journey in his search for distant lands, but he winds up
a short flight from home.
ISBN 1-888444-10-X
[1. Ducks—Fiction.]
I. Warnes, Tim, ill. II. Title.
PZ7. L51565DAV 1997 [E]—DC20 96-27750 CIP AC
Printed in Belgium
First American Edition
1 3 5 7 9 10 8 6 4 2

DAVY'S SCARY JOURNEY

by Christine Leeson

Pictures by Tim Warnes

Little Tiger Press

Davy Duckling lived with his mother
by a stream that flowed through a wood.

All summer long Davy paddled happily
in the water, but sometimes he watched
other birds flying high overhead and
wondered what lay beyond the trees.

As summer ended, Davy watched the
swallows gathering on the branches of
the trees. They seemed to be whispering
and planning among themselves.

"What are you doing up there?" he called.

"We're getting ready to fly away to warmer lands," said the swallows. "Winter is too cold for us here."

Davy sighed. He wished he could see new places, too.

"Can I come with you?" asked Davy.

"You?" laughed the oldest swallow.

"You could never keep up with us.
Our journey is too long and far too
dangerous. We will cross wide green seas where
sharks swim."

"We will swoop with the eagles over shining
mountain peaks," said another.

"We will cross fiery deserts of burning sand
before we reach the grassy plains," said a third.
"And the plains are no place for a little duckling.
You might get stepped on by a giraffe or eaten
by a lion."

Davy stuck his beak in the air. "All right then,
if you won't take me, I'll get there by myself—
you'll see!" he quacked.

The very next day Davy began his journey, paddling downstream toward the sea. Soon the stream left the trees and opened out into a misty stretch of rippling water. Davy could not see the other side.

"This must be the sea," he decided. "I hope there are no sharks here."

The sea was very wide, and although the waves were not high, Davy had to paddle for an awfully long time. It seemed that it would take him forever, but at last he saw land appearing ahead of him in the distance.

Davy rested for a while before setting out again, and it was sunset by the time he reached the foot of the mountains.

"They are bigger than I thought," he said as he began to climb. He could barely scramble over the huge rocks.

Night was falling as he reached the top of the mountain.

"Now all I have to do is to get down again," thought Davy. "I hope I don't meet one of those eagles on the way."

Davy's climb down did not take long as he slipped, slid, and bounced to the bottom. In front of him, beyond a tangle of grass, stretched the big desert! Strange shapes crouched in the darkness as Davy waddled out across the gravel and sand.

"This desert doesn't feel very fiery to me," thought Davy, "but those wild animals look scary. I just hope they don't pounce!"

Davy trudged on through the night.
As the first gleam of sunrise lit the sky,
he hauled himself to the top of a low hill
and saw the grassy plains stretching far ahead.
"I'm here! I've made it!" shouted Davy,
flapping his stubby little wings in excitement
as he ran down the hill and onto the plain.

Suddenly, Davy stopped and looked up.
Many pairs of very long legs towered
above him.

"What strange animals!" he gasped.
"They must be the giraffes the swallows
were talking about."

Davy scuttled back to the safety of a bush.
He wanted to settle down for a nice nap . . .

. . . but another animal was waiting
for him in the shadows—
a tawny-colored, yellow-eyed,
sharp-fanged one!

"A lion!" squeaked Davy,
backing away in fright.
    The lion crouched, tensed itself,
and leapt out of the bushes, right
on top of . . .

. . . Mother Duck!

"QUACK QUACK QUACK!" squawked
Mother Duck, pecking hard as she fought off
the fierce, spitting lion.

The lion
bristled and fled,
with Mother Duck
flapping after it.

"Well, I got rid of him!" said Mother Duck as
she came back. "It looks like I arrived just in time.
I've been searching for you all night, you naughty
duckling." She ruffled Davy's feathers. "And now
I think it's time you came home with me."

Davy agreed. He had seen enough of the world
for one day.

Davy hopped onto his mother's back,
and they flew high into the air.

"Oh look, Mother!"
cried Davy. "You can
see everything from
up here!"
And so they could—
the grassy plains, the fiery desert,
the mountains, and the sea.
"I went a long way, didn't I?" said Davy
proudly. "And the swallows haven't even
arrived yet!"